Pat,

May this little story
bring a smile
and a
tighter Divine Connection
for you and yours!

😊 Jane
12-20-16

CLARITY
OVER COFFEE

JAKE P. KNIGHT AND JANE G. KNIGHT

WESTBOW
PRESS®
A DIVISION OF THOMAS NELSON
& ZONDERVAN

THE HOLY BIBLE, NEW INTERNATIONAL VERSION®, NIV® Copyright © 1973, 1978, 1984, 2011 by Biblica, Inc.® Used by permission. All rights reserved worldwide.

Scripture taken from The Message. Copyright © 1993, 1994, 1995, 1996, 2000, 2001, 2002. Used by permission of NavPress Publishing Group.

Scripture taken from the King James Version of the Bible.

Scripture taken from the American Standard Version of the Bible.

WestBow Press books may be ordered through booksellers or by contacting:

WestBow Press
A Division of Thomas Nelson & Zondervan
1663 Liberty Drive
Bloomington, IN 47403
www.westbowpress.com
1 (866) 928-1240

ISBN: 978-1-5127-6219-8 (sc)
ISBN: 978-1-5127-6220-4 (e)

Library of Congress Control Number: 2016918083

Print information available on the last page.

WestBow Press rev. date: 11/16/2016

Dedication

To our beloved neighbors,
the dearly missed
Katherine King

and

Jim King
Two amazing human beings
who provided the inspiration for Katherine and Guy

ACKNOWLEDGEMENTS

As mom and son, we had a ball putting this little story together. We brainstormed, we wrote, we procrastinated, we shared insights, and we grew to know each other at a level beyond what either of us had imagined. And on this side of our experience, we still like each other!

Clarity Over Coffee began differently for each of us, and neither would claim it as "my" story. It's a blending of our experiences in learning to have ever-richer conversations with our Lord. We are grateful for every person along the way who has informed and is informing our understanding.

Thank you to our friends and family for reading our story, and a double thanks to those courageous enough to give us feedback: to Judy Yauch for her careful reading and coaching, and for identifying the title; to Blake Kersey for lending his biblical expertise; to Barbie Allen, Brenda Pangle, Darlene Ziegler, David Hatch, Doug Sittason, Eddie Allen, Gail Blumberg, Gail Sharpe, Greg Cain, Helen Russell, Jerry Busby, Jim King, Jim Ray, Joann Wotton, Jonathan Catherman, John Flokstra, Karen Knight, Katrina Hale, Larry Little, Lauren Little, Lynn Bornemann, Madge Hayes, Malissa Williams, Marcilla Weems, Mary Gregory, Melissa Jackson, Melissa Sittason, Melvin Russell, Michael Gentry, Michael Scott, Micki Jo'ell, Miriam Craig, Moriah Jarrett, Morgan Tolleson, Nell Chapman, Pat Crow, Paula Barnes, Peggy Busby, Regina Wright, Sandy Mathis, Sarah

Noble-Flokstra, Sara Etheridge, Shelly Rider, Suzanne Hays, Tessa Hollenbeck, and Tom Hewlett.

Finally, we offer thanks to our awesome spouses: Jerry and Marie. We love you for your patience, for your support, and perhaps for a few other reasons!

CHAPTER 1

How on earth can it possibly take more than one minute to download a five-page PDF file? There's not so much as a picture in the document, Kelli thought, feeling her brain pushing the boundaries of her skull.

Despite the sunny, crisp autumn morning and the intertwining aroma of percolating java and freshly baked pastries, Kelli found herself more frazzled by the minute. Since her home and office were teeming with distractions, Kelli had decided to begin frequenting Kat's Kafé before work to knock out some of the mindless paperwork before the day began in earnest. The coffee and cinnamon roll were delectable. *Maybe not the best breakfast idea, but we'll call it a cheat meal ... or day.* The mound of redundant text, however, was grating on her nerves. *Does an insurance claim for a fender bender actually require this much detail?*

"About time," she muttered to herself as legal jargon flooded the screen.

"About time for what?"

Startled from her carpal-tunnel vision, she raised her eyes to a kind face, smiling down on her with genuine inquiry. "Oh, this inane document finally downloaded, so I can forge further into my misery," Kelli said, immediately embarrassed by her own candor.

"Sounds to me like you might want to 'forge' in another direction," the kind face said as she pulled up a chair at Kelli's table.

"I was being a bit hyperbolic. It's just a bit early to indulge in the mundane, but I guess there's never a good time for that."

"True enough. I'm Katherine, by the way."

"Kelli," she said as her face began to ever so slightly relax into a smile.

"I'm sorry I just plopped down at your table like I own the place."

"You do," a faceless voice blurted from behind the counter.

"No, no, it's fine," Kelli said, welcoming the pleasant distraction. "So you actually do own the place?"

"Co-owner, technically. My husband and I bought this property from some friends a few years ago. Actually, we've owned it for about twenty-five years now. We continued to lease it to Bob's Sporting Goods until he ran out of room and built a new store. About that time, I decided I had had about enough lawyering, and Guy had been retired for about a decade, so we decided to try our hand at a small business."

Kat's Kafé sat nestled between a local artist's studio, Art's Art, and a boutique, Gidget's Gadgets, in the downtown Vestbrook suburb of Biggesttown, Alabama. The area, while always thriving, had recovered nicely from the overtly materialistic, chain-store rage of the '80s and '90s. Downtown Vestbrook now consisted of hipsters, young professionals, modern retirees, college students, and schoolchildren at virtually all times of the day.

"Ahh, so you can empathize with my frustrations." Kelli sighed.

"Are you also a retired lawyer who co-owns a coffeehouse with your doting husband?" Katherine asked, visibly proud of her sarcastic retort.

"All but the retired, coffeehouse, and doting husband part. I'm in the associate category at Jones, Schwartz, and Associates ... hence my frustration."

"From the looks of it, you don't have much to be frustrated about. You've managed to make a suit look both professional and cute. You appear to be in great shape. Your hair is gorgeous. And I bet there's no shortage of male suitors knocking at your door."

"I appreciate the confidence boost, but looks can be deceiving. I don't really feel like any of those are true. You, however, appear to have it going on. You've managed to dress cutely, professionally, and comfortably. You have this incredibly serene establishment. You hinted at a doting husband. And you are a retired lawyer! Looks to me like I need to pattern myself after you."

"Despite my humble nature, I can't deny any of that," Katherine said with a devilish grin. "But I wasn't always retired. I had my share of down periods, muddling through the waters of mundane, inane frustrations. But once you hit seventy, every day above ground is a good one."

"You're seventy?" Kelli asked, visibly shocked.

"Seventy-five, actually. And trust me, I feel every bit of it."

"You'll probably scoff at this, but thirty-one isn't exactly feeling exhilarating."

"Honestly, I can empathize there, too. That's right about the age I was forced to make some pretty heavy life-altering decisions. Looking back, I'm not sure why I was so frustrated." Katherine seemed to drift into the past for a moment.

"Then again, I do understand. I hated my job. My husband and I worked completely opposite schedules. I couldn't spend enough time with my kids. I was questioning my faith, and it was a turbulent time to live in Alabama. So, I made the obvious decision. I quit my job in pursuit of what I truly cared for."

"That's it?" Kelli asked, unimpressed. "If I quit, all my prayers are answered?"

"When you put it like that, it sounds easy. But I toiled for years, looked in every nook and cranny, talked to everyone I knew, and finally stumbled into a firm that fit my career goals. But I stumbled into that firm because I refused to settle for misery."

"That's so me right now. Do I want to shoot for a smaller firm, a larger firm with different interests, a corporate job—or do I want to duck out of law altogether? I've got so many options and interests rattling around in my head. I just don't know which one I should pursue."

"Basically, the massive overflow of ideas bombarding your brain is leaving you mentally paralyzed?"

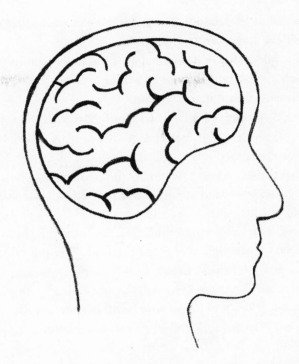

"Exactly! I look around and see so many people doing exactly what they love, living the perfect life. And here I am, flopping around in my bed every night, wrestling with every option available."

"Clarity is not coming easily, huh?"

"Not at all. I pray. I count sheep. I try falling asleep with the TV on. I try reading myself to sleep. Nothing works."

"You're bringing me back to my thirties," Katherine exclaimed. "I remember lying there miserable, just hoping."

"Oh, get over it," piped a raspy voice behind Kelli. "You're both young and energetic … Well, you're no spring chicken." The voice directed this statement at Katherine. "I'm ninety-two. It takes me fifteen minutes to get from my living room to my bathroom, thirty to walk to my mailbox, and a full hour to make it the quarter mile to get here. You two have nothing to complain about."

"Now, Mrs. Violet," Katherine said, "even a 'summer chicken' like myself can have some rough spots."

"You wouldn't know a rough spot if it slapped you in the nose. Summer chicken? Ha! Try dead of winter."

"Then where does that leave you?"

"Sugar, I've outlived all the seasons," Mrs. Violet said, visibly proud of this retort. "Can someone get me my sandwich? I ordered it twenty minutes ago."

Truth be told, Mrs. Violet had ordered her sandwich three minutes earlier. It seemed her grasp of time had escaped somewhere in the last decade or so.

"She gets a bit ornery sometimes." Katherine turned back to Kelli as Mrs. Violet continued to chastise the staff. "I've got an idea, but only if you want to hear it. Don't think I'm trying to pressure you."

"As long as it's not too involved. I've got enough going on."

"This will take a few weeks, and it will require some homework, but I promise it won't actually eat up too much of your time."

"Maybe."

"In the brief time we've been chatting, I've determined you to be a capable and resourceful young woman. I believe the answers to your frazzled and frustrating mental paralysis are inside you. May I challenge you to create a way to capture some of that wisdom?"

"Sounds a bit daunting, but I'm all ears."

"Start a journal," Katherine gently suggested. "Maybe on your phone or iPad, in an actual journal, or on a collection of cocktail napkins. The medium doesn't matter. Just spend about ten or fifteen minutes about three times over the next week. Explore who you are, where you are, where you're going, and how you want to get there. Maybe start with who you are, what you feel your life purpose is, and the major roles you are using to live that purpose."

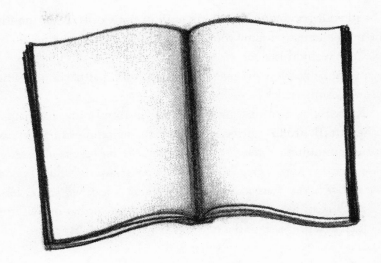

Kelli sat for a moment, giving this serious consideration.

"Okay, I'll think on it," Kelli said, looking at her phone. "Oooohh, I'd better go. I have a meeting in thirty minutes."

"I hope I didn't invade your space this morning. Sometimes I get a bit nosy," Katherine said.

"Not at all. It's nice knowing someone else has been where I am. I'll give some thought to your idea, and maybe even give it a shot."

As Kelli made her exit, Katherine's reflections on the conversation were short-lived as her doting husband made his traditional cheesy entrance.

"Honey, your man has once again, literally, brought home the bacon," Guy pronounced proudly as he meandered behind the counter.

"Sweetheart, it's not literal if it's not our home," Katherine said, easing back behind the counter. "I just met the sweetest young lady."

"I heard. Sounds like you've changed up your advice-giving strategy."

"You know I've always regretted the dogmatic way I used to push our kids."

"It wasn't as bad as you remember, but I do like how you've

refined your approach. You didn't push or put words in her mouth. She might actually follow your advice and return with some intel."

"You really think so?"

"I do, baby. Now get over there, and cook that bacon up. This man needs his vittles."

Roughly two miles away, sitting in mind-numbing, stop-and-go traffic, Kelli noticed she lacked the agitation of her typical morning commute. *I actually feel better. Katherine appears to actually understand my plight. I really am mentally paralyzed right now. Nice to have a diagnosis. That's it. Tonight I designate fifteen minutes to this.*

With that, Kelli allowed an angry driver to cut her off without so much as a grimace, and a new day began.

CHAPTER 2

One week to the day later, Kelli crept into Kat's with guarded excitement. In the days since her first encounter with Katherine, she had experienced two potentially life-changing realizations. Sunday's church service sparked the first as her pastor began a series on using the Lord's Prayer as a structure or model for personal prayer. This also prompted her to dig out her leadership training materials from a course she had taken in her senior year in college to assist with this new idea.

However, she had also begun wondering if she really needed to put her trust in a stranger. If so, would said stranger actually follow through appropriately? Kelli wanted to trust Katherine. Thoughts of gaining a coach to walk with her through struggles held definite appeal, but self-preservation and independence were two stalwarts she had become fond of over the past few years.

Life had taken several twists she had not anticipated, leading her to trust only in herself and her family. Boyfriends had never panned out. Friends were fickle. Colleagues were ultimately selfish. Time and time again, life had proven one thing to Kelli: the only person she could count on was herself.

Last week, Katherine had caught her with one foot off the merry-go-round. Kelli had let her guard down and exposed her inner self to a stranger, and here she was returning for more? *This will not happen twice!*

Besides, what's to say this lady will even be here or remember me?
Okay, one cup of coffee, maybe a light breakfast, and then it's off to …

"Kelli!" Katherine exclaimed with genuine enthusiasm and a mouthful of what could only be a blueberry scone.

I should have just stayed home, Kelli thought. *New plan: fake busy and never cross this threshold again.*

"I was hoping you'd make it in today. I need your advice on a legal matter."

This was exactly why Kelli had built these defenses. People always wanted something for free. People always wanted to use her for something.

"Could I be sued for creating the most amazing scone on the planet? The divinity of these tasty pastries may create an addiction to rival the nastiest of the narcotics realm."

"Hmmmmmm … As of now, you are in danger. I see no disclaimer posted, nor was I warned of the addictive properties of said pastry upon ordering it during my last visit. If you would like to avoid future litigation, contact my secretary to set up an appointment."

This woman was good. Within seconds, yet again, Kelli found herself disarmed, defenses down, bridge laid across the moat. Plan B scratched. On to plan C: proceed with surface issues *only!*

"Best scones on the planet?" Mrs. Violet piped in. "It's not even the best scone on this street."

"Mrs. Violet, nobody else serves scones on this street," Katherine retorted.

"That's my point."

"You're too sweet, Mrs. Violet."

"Just telling the truth … Hey y'all aren't going to have one of those namby-pamby 'what-does-it-all-mean' conversations again, are you?" Mrs. Violet snorted, using the quotation fingers.

Before Katherine could respond, Mrs. Violet turned her attention to a well-dressed man in the neighboring seat and began third-degree interrogation of his personal affairs.

"Thank goodness he's tolerant," Katherine said to Kelli. "That should buy us at least five minutes without interruption. How's that journal looking?"

Kelli begrudgingly began to pull the journal out of her bag before Katherine stopped her.

"I don't want to read it, sweetheart—I just want to know how it's affecting your psyche."

"Well, um … I feel like I've laid some significant things firmly out there, but there's no real resolution."

Maybe it wouldn't be a horrible thing to open up a bit to Katherine. What's the worst that could happen?

Without divulging too much, Kelli described her pastor's series on personalizing the Lord's Prayer and incorporating her learning from her leadership training.

She was beginning to think these two concepts might form the perfect storm for streamlining her own existence.

Once church had wrapped up on Sunday, Kelli had found herself knee-deep in her old college materials, sifting through memories and realizing how smart she actually was at one point. After forty-five minutes of diligent searching, she had come across her leadership training materials. Her learning guide was intact and in more detail than she had remembered. She found her former roles and mission quite intriguing, but it was certainly time to give them an overhaul.

Six solid roles emerged as she revamped her list in the how-to-live-your-life section of her guide.

The first consisted of her relationship with God. She had always liked the concept of his most excellent harmonies (Phil. 4:9, MSG). Something about that phrase made her smile. In her mind, all the people of the world, the angels in heaven, and God himself were performing a sing-along to rival the best sing-alongs of all time. And the song was more than music; it was the cycle of seasons, the ecology of plants and animals, the harmonies produced by differences in people, and so much more. The entire world in harmony? Yup, that was going in role one, and she would participate as "his instrument," ready to perform her parts.

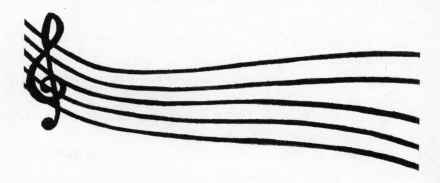

Role two took a slightly more wishful turn. To this point in her life, no one had presented himself as Mr. Right. Despite this, however, she held out hope that he would amble across her path and woo her as no other had been wooed before, and they would make babies and live happily ever after. Therefore, she titled this role "soulmate."

To identify herself as daughter, sister, cousin, niece, etc., she simply titled role three "family member." Kelli constantly found her attentions tugged and stretched between work, friends, and family. Most of the time, family won out, and she aimed to keep that trend afloat by giving this role its due.

Next on the list had to be "friend." Kelli loved people and found a lot of joy and satisfaction being a good friend. Role four, check.

Role five fell under the work category, but she wanted a descriptor that communicated more than that. As a result, she wound up with the title "advocate" to integrate her work with her career, as well as community organizations and church.

Finally, she felt the call to be a better neighbor. Not just to the people who lived close to her, but to all she came in contact with who did not fall into the friend, relative, or colleague categories. Role six then became "neighbor."

"In a nutshell, I guess what I'm creating is a comprehensive and personal pattern for my daily conversations with God."

"So you plan on boring God with the same old prayer every night?" Mrs. Violet chimed in.

"I hope not," Kelli kindly responded. "I'm just realizing that every time I pray, I essentially say the same things in a sloppy fashion. Using this approach seems more respectful and effective. I'm simply looking for a way to open my day with him, to connect, to start a divine conversation that, in a very real way, can last all day long."

"Wow," Katherine said with raised eyebrow. "When you left last week, I was just hoping you'd return with a solid thought or two, but you've exceeded anything I was considering."

"Yeah," Kelli responded, "I tend to obsess a bit when I start something. Truth is, I sporadically thought about what we'd discussed until Sunday, when my preacher hit me with the 'aha' moment."

"I love the idea of personalizing the Lord's Prayer. I haven't exactly done that with my prayers, but mine are kind of similar. I start with the base of what I feel I need to tell God and thank him for every day. Then I add bullet points, so to speak, at the end to tie up any loose ends for the day."

"If you ask me, you're both overthinking it," Mrs. Violet said, horning in further. "All you have to do is close your eyes, tell the Big Guy what you need to tell him, and move on."

"Well, Mrs. Violet, you've got your way, I've got mine, and Kelli is tweaking hers. Is that so bad?"

"Is my sandwich ready yet? Don't you overcook it like you did last time. I thought I was chewing on a dried-up sponge," Mrs. Violet said, turning her attentions to her needs of the flesh.

"So far, I've just tackled the first three phrases," Kelli said, refocusing the conversation with Katherine, "and I have to admit, I'm kind of excited about it."

"I know. Your face is more relaxed, and you're quite a bit more hopeful than last week."

"It's that obvious, huh?" Kelli said, deciding to open up a bit more. "My pastor suggested last Sunday to use the first part of the Lord's Prayer, 'Our Father in heaven, hallowed be your name,' to explore and meditate on my relationship with him. This week I focused on who he is and who I am in relation to him."

"It appears you're quite comfortable with how that's working."

"Oddly enough, I am. I know I'll never have it all figured out, but there's something to be said for putting my feelings about my life into words. That simple task has added a relative amount of clarity."

"Are you going to work on it every day?"

"I have a goal of three days a week, like we said. But if I go over, that's fine. On some days, I expect I'll keep this routine fairly short and sweet. On others, it may go on and on, but on all days, I want it to be very real with a definite conversational twist.

"And I'm really liking your idea to modernize as well as personalize. Again, I am deeply impressed with how far you've taken this," Katherine said, welling with pride.

"Thanks. It all feels right, you know?"

"Sounds to me like your mental paralysis is subsiding."

"Exactly! I can now wiggle my big toe.

"I have been a bit more at ease this week and am more cognizant of my actions. I'm thinking my next step is to clarify my life purpose.

Though I created one for my leadership training, it doesn't feel quite right. I'm not sure it captures what God is calling me to be and do."

"And the struggle returns to your face."

"Yup."

"What do you want that statement to do for you?"

"Good question. I suppose I want it to lead and inspire me to participate fully in 'his most excellent harmonies.'" (Phil. 4:9 MSG).

"Would you like another challenge?"

Kelli consented, hoping this wouldn't be too involved.

"From what I have deciphered, you developed your current statement with some heavy thought. It very well might hold the essence of your calling. Play with the wording and see where it takes you."

With a legitimate smile on her face, Kelli realized how lucky she was to have happened into this particular coffee destination.

"I hate to cut this off, but legal duty calls."

"I have some pastry booty to whip up myself. I'd love it if you found yourself back in here fairly soon. I can't wait to see how the prayer progresses."

"It might be a few days, but I'll get back here when I can. Thanks for lending your ear and your prompts."

"No problem, sweetie. You have a good week."

"You too."

"She's serious about defeating this mental paralysis, huh?" Guy asked knowingly.

"You're getting pretty good at this eavesdropping," Katherine said, making her way back behind the counter.

"This new advice-giving strategy has me intrigued."

"I know it's only our second conversation, and it's probably none of my business, but I just can't help myself. Am I being too forward with her?"

"Not at all. She's looking for guidance, and you seem to be providing it in a most unobtrusive fashion."

"She is taking inventory of who she is and how she is contributing. I'm really impressed with the intellectual and prayerful energy she's investing by cloaking her words around her calling. Naming her roles and the major ways she contributes is genius."

"You are guiding this one well, my dear."

"Hardly; she's doing all the work. I'm just asking her about it."

"Exactly!"

Meanwhile, amidst the cacophony of interstate traffic and her favorite music app, Kelli likened the noise to God's symphony, with her as his instrument playing the parts of soulmate, family member, friend, advocate, and neighbor—all parts in his harmonies.

Then it hit, the "aha" moment. Her life's calling could be summed up in this way: "his instrument to accompany authentic living and divine engagement in my circles of influence."

Kelli's prayer begins ...

*"Our Father in heaven, hallowed be your name"
(Matt. 6:9 NIV). Creator, Eternal Father, God the
Father, God the Son, God the Holy Spirit. What does
that mean? Who am I to honor you? But, then, who
am I not to?*

*You created me. You know me. You love me. You've
accepted me into your eternal family (John 3:16 NIV).
You invite me to join your most excellent harmonies
(Phil. 4:9 MSG). You call me to accompany authentic
living and divine engagement, to be your instrument
playing the parts of soulmate, family member, friend,
advocate, and neighbor.*

CHAPTER 3

"Have you found a man yet?" Mrs. Violet belted out before Kelli's glutes could hit the chair.

"I find men every day," Kelli replied without thinking.

"You know what I mean. I don't see a ring. I'm just wondering if you've got anyone."

"No."

"Well, what's the holdup? You're young, pretty, smart …" Mrs. Violet tailed off as if she had forgotten where she was. "You need a man."

"Mrs. Violet, she'll get a man when she's good and ready. Won't you, sugar?" Katherine popped in from nowhere.

Truth was, Kelli didn't just want a man, she wanted *the* man. Periodically, she found herself caught up in the ultimate cliché of popcorn and Lifetime movies, sobbing for no reason, but overall, she wasn't pining. She liked the marital concept but had yet to get around to it.

"Any 'aha' moments this week?" Katherine said.

"How about this for my life's calling: 'I am his instrument to accompany authentic living and divine engagement in all of my circles.'"

"Jackpot!"

"Between the sweet sounds of Highway I-37 and my favorite music app, it hit me when I left here last week."

"Your tone tells me that wasn't quite enough to ease your worried mind."

"While I have upgraded the Lord's Prayer from a template to an investigative guide, I'm stuck on what it means for me to be 'on earth as it is in heaven'." "There's just no way for me to reach heavenly perfection."

"One guy did that, and he was persecuted for it," Mrs. Violet popped in. "You might've heard of him? His name was Jesus! You act like you've never picked up a Bible."

As Mrs. Violet continued to detail the story of the crucifixion, Katherine and Kelli patiently waited, wheels turning in both brains.

"I think she's well aware of that, Mrs. Violet. Kelli is just trying to wrap her head around striving for perfection, not attaining it."

"Sounds like a semantical goose chase to me," Mrs. Violet retorted before calling out, "Marcolio, sandwich!"

Katherine redirected the conversation back to Kelli. "So, perfection is not the objective, and the objection to perfection is not the direction. It's the pursuit of perfection that guides you in the right direction."

"Um ..." Kelli said, processing rhyme-master Katherine's words. "Are you a poet?"

"I've dabbled, but I must say, that was one of my better impromptu statements. I always wanted to give some Sharpton-esque closing argument in trial, but never quite summoned the courage."

"I'm not the only one? I used to fantasize about dealing out a rhythmic fifteen-minute closing argument ending with a thunderous standing ovation from a packed court room led by the judge."

"Now, that's the ticket!"

"There I go again. This is the kind of stuff I think about all day, not the stuff that matters."

"What's so bad about that? Our best ideas spring forth when the abjectly absurd flows through our minds.

"Speaking of which, give me more on that investigative guide."

"I'm looking, or rather investigating, other Scripture to deepen my understanding of his word and how to incorporate it into my life."

"Do I detect a movement back toward that impossible thing called perfection?"

"I recognize I don't have to understand heaven to know how to personalize my concept of it. That's what I am investigating.

When I get stuck or intrigued by a word or phrase, I go looking for additional insight."

"What have you found to help you understand 'as it is in heaven'?"

"I'm still searching. I remember my pastor saying the first part of the Lord's Prayer is about the relationship with God. Simple enough. Recognize God, that he and I have a unique relationship, and that I can bring honor to him in all my being and doing. But, how can I live my calling 'as it is in heaven' if I don't have a clear picture of heaven?"

"Oh, for heaven's sake!" a now wildly agitated Mrs. Violet belted. "Leave it to you lawyers to over-think something so simple. Just make like Peter and get out of the boat. Jesus didn't facilitate any 'what does it all mean' jibber-jabber. He just told Peter to get out of the boat."

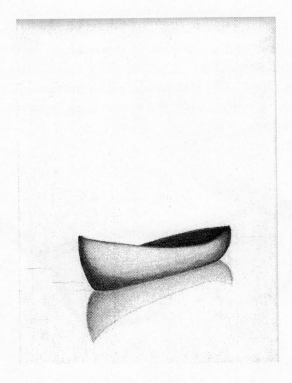

"But what do I do after I get out of this boat? Swim?"

"Have you even been to church? Jesus didn't ask Peter to understand. He just asked Peter to get out of the boat and look at him."

"The lady may be onto something. As long as Peter kept his eyes on Jesus, he stayed on top of the water. What does that say?"

"Well ... he wants us to look to him. He is God the Son, the Living Word, my example of a life lived perfectly in love. Everything in heaven exudes love and faith. He wants me to look to him, to continuously ask and listen."

"Sounds like we're hitting some 'aha' moments," Katherine said proudly.

"It would appear Mrs. Violet brought the 'aha' hammer today. Time for me to investigate and think on Peter's walk."

"Looks like you've got your thought of the week to chew on."

"That I do. Sure would be nice to have some face-to-face Jesus coaching like Peter had, though. How in the world can I figure this out all by myself? I just don't have the vision to see through the murky world lens."

"Here," Mrs. Violet said, handing Kelli her glasses. "Try these. They're strong enough to see a nose hair of the man on the moon in broad daylight."

It's quite strange where "aha" moments come from sometimes, but this little nugget hit the nail on the head. Mrs. Violet was one hundred percent correct. The key wasn't in figuring out the meaning behind every little detail, and the reality was, that wasn't humanly possible. The key was in staying focused on the most important detail, the most important One.

Moments after Kelli began her daily commute, Guy provided more evidence of his ever-improving eavesdropping skills.

"Now we have Mrs. Violet bringing the heat? This is turning into quite a show."

"I know. Looks like I'm getting the hang of it too. I wish I'd had Kelli's insight when back in my thirties."

"Me too."

"Hey, you weren't supposed to agree to that."

"Truth is, your insight got us where we got a lot quicker than my insight would have gotten us. You pushed for the smaller house and the cheaper car and the coach flights and the mid-range hotels and all the little steps that helped us jump ahead earlier than any of our friends. Oh yeah, and you found the perfect church family for us. And that was before you hit thirty."

"I guess I was pretty awesome," Katherine said with a sly grin.

"And you still are, my love."

On the commuting side of town, Kelli found herself astounded at Mrs. Violet's insight.

I'm not the maestro leading the symphony, Kelli thought. *I'm merely a player following his lead. That certainly turns perception from the scary murky to the peaceful.*

Kelli's prayer continues ...

I am your instrument participating in your song, your symphony, your work.

Your kingdom come, your will be done on earth— through me today—as it is in heaven (Matt.6:10 NIV). What does that mean for me today? Will I be playing loudly or softly? I don't know what this part of the song sounds like, and my human eyes can't read the music. I know who and what are on my agenda, but I don't know what the people in my life need to hear from you through me today. That is really fuzzy. It is such a stretch for me to see myself functioning as I would in heaven, where every single thought, word, and action surely come from love—genuine, selfless, divine love.

So I step into this day the way Peter stepped out of the boat: with his attentions firmly fixed on you,

Jesus—God the Son, the Living Word, the only life lived perfectly in love—he walked confidently on water. His challenge actually became the foundation for his walk. With my attention on you and alert to the passions, intuition, and insights prompted by you, Holy Spirit (John 20:22 NIV), I will walk confidently in my calling today, and my challenging distractions will be mitigated to background music for my parts in your glorious harmonies (Phil. 4:9 MSG).

CHAPTER 4

Daily bread, Kelli thought as she strolled toward morning bliss in a cup.

How could that possibly translate to modern times?

For one thing, she was trying to avoid gluten despite the new "organic" bakery on Fourth Street. The concept had vexed her all week. Not that she was actually taking it literally, but she just couldn't quite narrow the concept down into a way to talk about it with God. On the average day, she needed food, water, shelter, the vast assortment of personal hygiene products, a car, electronic devices, empathy, toughness, skill, sleep, bathrooms ... how could she ask for all that in just a couple of lines?

Only Marco welcomed Kelli from behind the counter on this

Tuesday morning. In case you're wondering, yes, he did live up to his name. This guy could grace the cover of any racy novel with ease, putting Fabio to shame. Sadly, however, he was a mere twenty-two, working toward his English degree, at which point he would cross the Pacific to bestow the wonders of his native language onto Korean youth and undoubtedly settle down with a bohemian local.

Regardless, he was easy on the eyes and not a bad conversationalist.

With a knowing glance and a "Good morning," Marco headed to the urn to prepare Kelli's usual.

"I don't need a lot in this world," Mrs. Violet's disembodied voice squawked, "but at this moment, toilet paper is topping the list."

"I told you I needed to put some in there," Katherine responded. "You couldn't wait two minutes."

"Two more minutes and ..."

With her morning order in place, Kelli nestled into the corner of the retro leather couch, pulled out her tablet, and fired it up.

"You're in my shop and you search for 'bread'?" Katherine chirped from behind Kelli's left shoulder.

"Not for sustenance. More like, 'Give us this day …' I'm just struggling to figure out the difference between needs and wants. Do I really need a car? A house? The types of food I consume?"

"It all depends on the moment. Right now, Mrs. Violet needs toilet paper …"

"No, now I need my sandwich I ordered thirty minutes ago."

"See? A perfect example. Our needs change throughout our lives. They change by the minute. We can't possibly predict what we need," Kelli mused.

"I can. I need food, clothes, shelter, and a bathroom with toilet paper. Give me that, and I'll survive the rapture."

"I wish it were that simple. How much specificity does he want from me? Do I ask God for everything? How specific? What am I not asking for now that I should or shouldn't?"

"You've put words around your life purpose-slash-calling. How might that impact the way you think about needs?" Katherine asked.

"To paraphrase Mrs. Violet, I'm making this too complicated. I'm just a bit baffled as to how I think through all the mundane details of my day-to-day life."

"Can you streamline the process a bit?"

"Four, maybe?" Kelli said, perking up. "I can group my entire life into four areas: physical—health, wellness, energy, and stamina; mental—ideas, fluency, and focus; social or emotional—peace and fun; spiritual—close walk with God."

Katherine sat back, apparently taking in the concept of four through her nose. After a few oxygen-enriching breaths, Katherine was on the same page.

"You can fit all of your roles—your life, actually—into those four categories?"

"Yes, at least I think I can," Kelli said. "They take care of body, mind, and spirit with the added bonus of relationships with others and myself.

"Perhaps I'll insert a long-time favorite verse from Philippians to sum up all that I need, paraphrasing something like: all that I need to be true, noble, right, pure, lovely, admirable, excellent, and praiseworthy."

"Sounds like you've got your 'daily bread' figured out."

"I sure would like my daily bread," Mrs. Violet barked as Marco placed the sandwich on her table.

And there it was. Mrs. Violet's grumpiness had unveiled another piece of the puzzle. *That sandwich was landing in front of her at the time it did no matter what Mrs. Violet said,* Kelli realized. *In the meantime, she could have chosen to read, watch television, carry on a nice conversation with a fellow customer, or gripe loudly till her sustenance became available. The "daily bread" is going to arrive. God is going to take care of the needs. Just focus on what's attainable at the moment and enjoy.*

"I cured you of eavesdropping today," Katherine said as Guy entered with two sacks full of produce.

"Do I at least get the summary of today's session?"

"I guess," Katherine said as she sorted through the bags. "Kelli has lumped her entire life into four categories: physical, mental, social or emotional, and spiritual."

"What part of the prayer does that wrap up?"

"Daily bread. She's translated 'daily bread' to encompass all aspects God provides."

"Any more brilliance from our favorite senior citizen?"

While Katherine explained Mrs. Violet's unwitting contribution to today's session, Kelli sat amazed that such an innocuous happening as Mrs. Violet getting her sandwich had sparked such a revelation. God would provide all she needed. All she had to do was ask him, trust him, follow her calling, and keep her eyes open.

Kelli's prayer continues ...

I want to play my parts today with loving grace and elegance. I look to you to give me all I need to do that, including health, wellness, energy, stamina, ideas, fluency, focus, peace, fun, and an intimate relationship with you (Matt. 6:11 NIV). All that I need to have only those thoughts, conversations, and behaviors that are true, noble, right, pure, lovely, admirable, excellent, and praiseworthy. I want to think on these things and practice these things, and I can with you (Phil. 4:8-9 NIV).

CHAPTER 5

Wednesday morning. Not the best time to hit Kat's Kafé for a relaxing start to the morning. One corner consisted of a sixth-grade girls' early morning discipleship group. A female teen church group inhabited another corner—the couch corner, Kelli's favorite spot. The rest of the tables were taken by a variety of couples, business meetings, and a host of friendly, breakfasting customers.

Coffee attained, order placed. The only option left was the high tables. Not the most comfortable, but there was space enough to enjoy the morning.

Collecting her thoughts proved impossible. Five feet behind her sat the teen group. It is a little-known fact, but the female species of the teenage ilk can be quite loud, especially when surrounded by its own.

"Grab an apron and get back here," Katherine piped over the noise. "We're at defcon four."

Kelli didn't even get the chance to respond. Katherine whisked around the corner and into the sixth-grade lair with maternal grace, ensuring every child had her caffeinated beverage of choice ... *That explains it!* Emily, Kelli's former roommate and a current sixth-grade teacher, could never figure out why her girls were so ridiculous on Wednesday mornings. *One quick text, and Emily now knows what she's battling.*

"What's on your agenda this morning?" Katherine asked.

"I thought you were still ..."

"Think about it, and I'll catch it on my next fly by."

"And God blessed us with free will," (Gal. 5:13-15 MSG) a well-spoken teen blared from the fluffy couch section.

Oh yeah, Kelli thought, *free will? Free will isn't free ... what is that supposed to mean, anyway? No, that's just Bob Dylan crooning amid the cacophony of Kat's Kafé. It is free, but one has to handle it properly.*

That's it, huh? Just give the people what they want? Kelli had been trying to give the people what they wanted her entire life and found herself woefully short in all attempts. At least, that was how she viewed it. She could give just enough to satisfy, but never enough to fill the obligation perfectly.

"Free will," Kelli said as Katherine blew by in a blur.

"On it, dear."

Yes, God would take care of her basic needs, but free will insinuated some responsibility on the part of the human.

"Free will isn't free."

"That's just Bob Dylan talking," Kelli said, proud she'd already cracked that particular code.

"Huh, I guess you're right. How does free will tie into … yes, honey. I'll have Mandy bring that right out to you."

Katherine was truly amazing. At one point, Kelli swore she was talking to five customers, retrieving a scone from the display, holding a latte, benevolently commanding her staff, and talking to a vendor on the phone.

"How do you do it all?" Kelli asked on the next fly-by.

"This? All I'm doing is giving people what they want."

"Welcome to the circus," a kind, southern, male voice lilted.

Kelli shifted her eyes from the digital box up to quite possibly the most content man she had ever laid eyes on.

"Sorry, I'm Guy, Katherine's husband. I noticed her dropping words in your direction and figured you must be the famous Kelli."

"It's great to finally meet you. I hope I haven't been a bother to her."

"Not at all. She loves people, and you've climbed pretty high on her list as of late."

"High praise," Kelli said, a bit embarrassed but equally grateful. "I just stumbled in here one day and unloaded my problems, and she picked them right up."

"That's her MO. Not to horn in on this, but she did share a few details of your plight. May I lend an ear while Katherine is otherwise occupied?"

"Of course," Kelli said, thrilled about getting to know Guy. "I'm working on incorporating a bit of a leadership seminar I attended into my prayer, but I have to admit I'm starting to wonder if this is just complicating things even more. It feels like I might be diluting instead of clarifying."

"It may seem like that, but think back to your first year out of law school."

They sat silent for a moment as Kelli recounted the mass of confusion that was her first professional job.

"Now, think about the last year of your professional life."

After another moment Kelli nodded.

"I see your point, but it's so hard to know for sure if I'm on the right track."

"It all starts with making the best choice with the information you have at the time," Guy said. "You have to constantly take initiative every moment of every day to achieve your best self. Sounds daunting, but like anything else, it just takes a bit of time and stick-to-it-ness."

"The problem lies in making the right choice," Kelli said. "In a roundabout way, it brings to mind 'take my yoke upon you,' which to me means be interdependent with him.

"To paraphrase the Message interpretation: walk with him, work with him, and watch how he does it. Learn from him the unforced rhythms of grace. That is a good choice, right?"

"Absolutely." Guy nodded with an affirming smile. "Now, how do you picture your life events as you walk, work, watch, and learn? Keep in mind, 'Where there is no vision, the people perish.'"

"Currently, I guess I don't. Instead, the day just kind of happens. But I could choose differently. I could choose to picture or envision— prayerfully—the outcomes and consequences of what I think, say, and do.

"Y'all really are quite the couple." Kelli broke off topic, amazed at her first conversation with Guy.

"I'm punching way out of my weight class, but she lets me hang around," Guy said with a mischievous smile.

"Actually, the keys to our longevity have been listening to each other, having meaningful conversations, and being present in the moment with each other."

"Why does that not surprise me? The more I try to hone that skill, the more I see others failing miserably. My boss, bless his heart, is constantly judging my clients before he even meets them. I feel like I'm constantly defending them to him. Okay, maybe that's good practice for the courtroom, but it still bothers me."

"Not like this happened overnight, but I found the more I put listening into practice, the more it rubbed off on my employees and even my friends," Guy offered. "Not so much on family, but those are the hardest to convert."

"No kidding. I'm still a ways away from listening as much as I would like, though."

"Like anything else, what's the quickest way to Carnegie Hall?"

"Practice," Kelli said, a bit excited to finally have that question posed to her.

"What can you gain from honing your listening skills?"

"Listening is critical to understanding and literally forms the basis for relationships."

"Nailed it. Without relationships, we have nothing. No career, no family, no friends, no spirituality."

"My professional tendencies sometimes get in the way of that understanding type of communication. I always regret when I'm a bit dogmatic, but at times, I think I have to be."

"No doubt," Guy said. "You're going to slip up and be dogmatic at times when it's not appropriate. The important thing is not that you act accordingly in every situation, but that you are aware of how you acted, so you can fix it next time by if need be."

"My kindergarten teacher would score me a 'needs improvement' in that category. I can self-berate with the best of them."

"Think constructive criticism. It's healthy for you to evaluate situations once you're out of them. Just don't wish for a time machine, because even if we had them, they would fix nothing."

"You think so?"

"The older you get, the more you realize regret does nothing but tear you apart. Just focus on what you can control when you can control it. Don't worry about all the junk you can't control."

"Wow," Kelli said, "I feel a little tighter just hearing that."

"It's like yoga for the brain," Guy said. "Now, take a look around."

At that moment, Katherine continued her orchestration, but most of the communication was sans verbiage. The chef was chefing, the cashier was cashiering, the waitresses were waitressing, and Katherine was diving in with whoever needed help whenever they needed it.

"Is there a way you can think of to put words around this chaos?" Guy mused.

"Everyone is completing his or her job and flexing his or her skills, and your wife is seamlessly floating from need to need without interrupting anyone's flow. Is this not a prime example of 'his most excellent harmonies'?"

"Exactly. Are any of them thinking about the economy or worried that a sinkhole might open under this establishment and swallow us all?"

"Nope. Each and every one of them is focused on what he or she can control at this very moment. As a result, they are collectively delivering quality service."

"I believe we have successfully solved the world's problems today. I hate to do this, but I have a budget committee meeting on the first tee in a little bit. It was an honor to finally meet you."

"Retirement sounds so nice."

"Be patient, and enjoy the ride you're on now."

"I'll do my best. Thank you."

Later that afternoon, as Guy eased into post-golf mode and Katherine reveled in the glow of her sunroom, they rehashed the morning conversation.

"Good thing I called in my self-leadership guns today," Katherine said.

"She did most of the heavy lifting," Guy responded. "I love the way she's using it as a tool kit for her spiritual life."

"That girl is sharp."

"The ideas she came up with just amazed me. She claimed to be fogged with confusion, but in reality, she was on the brink of clarity. Maybe she's not quite there, but seems to me she's pretty close."

"I have to say, she's way ahead of where we were at her age."

Meanwhile, in commuter's paradise, Kelli didn't quite feel ahead of the game, but she felt an odd state of bliss was setting in as she thought about her progress.

Of course, none of this is set in stone, she thought. *It's not like I'm creating the Ten Commandments here, but it fits me right now.*

Kelli's prayer continues ...

Not as a puppet waiting for you to pull my strings, but with you. You have set me free, giving me freedom of choice (Gal. 5:13-15 MSG). I am free to choose my thoughts, words, and actions, and today I choose to partner with you. I choose to walk with you, work with you, and watch how you do it. I choose to learn from you the unforced rhythms of grace (Matt. 11:28-30 MSG).

I choose to partner with you in exercising vision— anticipating outcomes, results, and consequences of what I think, say, and do, and in forming the next right piece of the picture of my calling (Pro. 29:18 KJV).

I choose to partner with you in focusing and executing my calling today, taking your love in and giving it all away (Matt. 6:30-33 MSG); in loving and forgiving dynamically with a generous spirit (2 Cor. 9:8-11 MSG), knowing you will provide everything I need—all the resources, even time—to play my parts throughout this day with excellence, elegance, and grace (Luke 12:25-32 MSG).

Partnering with you today, I choose to be fully present, listening with genuine consideration and sharing my perceptions with courage—even bold courage—as appropriate (Acts 17:22-31 MSG). I choose to celebrate what's right with people and work with them to share authentic gifts and bents (Rom. 12:4-5 MSG).

And, partnering with you today, I choose to grow—gracefully and continuously—in all facets of my life (Luke 2:52 NIV).

CHAPTER 6

Kat's was wrought with tension when Kelli entered the following Tuesday. She was so proud of herself for getting up early, knowing Wednesdays were way too much for her to take. But now, she kind of regretted waking up. Probably not a good day to have a cup of joe and a leisurely conversation.

Too late to turn back now. She went through the café routine, read through her prayer to date, and started thinking about "forgive us our debts" (Matt. 6:12 NIV).

"I don't expect you to be perfect, Marco," Kelli overheard Katherine saying from the back. "But I do expect you to get here on time. The youth thing is not an excuse. Here in the real world, you're either where you're supposed to be when you're supposed to be or you're not. Today you were not. Last Thursday and Friday you were not. This is the last documented warning. Do you understand?"

While the thickness of the walls was a bit lacking, Kelli still felt guilty for listening in.

Marco slinked from the back and reassumed his post. Minutes later, a chipper Katherine emerged.

"What a Tuesday gift," Katherine exclaimed, completely befuddling Kelli. "I felt so bad that we weren't able to talk last week, but it sounds like Guy did far better than I could have."

Kelli immediately looked to Marco, noticing his demeanor was right back to his easy-going, happy self.

"Oh, honey, did you overhear that? I'm so sorry. I didn't think anyone was sitting here."

"I shouldn't have been …"

"You didn't know. And these walls just barely block the view. A good gust of wind would give us a completely open floor plan.

"Everything's fine. I just had to let him know how things are going to work once he's using his degree. I love the boy to death, but that won't stop me from teaching him the right way. In fact, that's why I bother."

"Did you set this up? The more I come in here, the more I wonder if you've got some grand scheme to direct me. Or am I just being narcissistic?"

"Wrong on both counts. Guy did tell me things unfolded rather conveniently in your visit last week. I tend to think, however, we see what we need to see when we need to see it. If you had not been thinking in that direction, you never would have noticed any of it."

"I never thought of it that way. But how do you explain my thinking about forgiveness all the way over here, and I walk in to you forgiving Marco for his 'debts,' or lack thereof?"

"Fate and destination? Sounds like the good Lord is leading you 'not into temptation.'"

"One thing at a time, please."

"Sorry, I couldn't help myself. I forgave Marco his 'debts' because I know what a great person he is and what a great man he is going to be. Were he a ne'er-do-well, and I have employed one or two of those in the past, I would still forgive him because of my beliefs, but he'd have to hit the ranks of the unemployed."

"But 'forgive us our debts' implies a bit more than proper work behavior, don't you think?

"That's what I've been chewing on this past couple of days. To me, it's all the things we think, say, and do that we shouldn't and all the things we don't think, say, and do that we should and the wrong beliefs and perceptions underneath that prompt our wrong behaviors."

"You have really been thinking about this. Sounds like that pretty much covers the definition. What's the next step?"

"Asking forgiveness in earnest. As in actually improving, altering, and growing."

"Or you could just ask forgiveness and not do that crap you did again." Mrs. Violet reentered the conversation with raging bluntness. "You two sound like Socrates and Plato minus the intellect."

"Mrs. Violet. You're a bit crotchety this morning."

"I'm crotchety every morning, but I'm always right. I've been around too long not to know everything."

"Seems a bit presumptuous."

"How about you grant me my sandwich, Marcum?" Mrs. Violet

raised and redirected her voice towards the counter. Kelli had heard every variation of Marc come out of her mouth, but never Marco.

"I used to correct her, but now we place bets on which name she'll call him next. Nobody won the day she dropped 'Marceroni.'

"But back to the topic at hand. Marco accepting and forgiving Mrs. Violet for never getting his name right is an example of ..."

"Divine love," Kelli had that answer on cue. "Forgiveness is an expression of divine love.

"Then it's on to temptation. Which sounds simple enough. We know to avoid wrath, greed, sloth, pride, lust, envy, and gluttony. But the phrase 'lead us not into temptation' shifts the onus onto God. Which is fine, but I'm to share in that burden."

"Perhaps it's the 'not' that bothers you?"

"Ok, how about, 'help me to be my best self,' which connotes my conscious effort to avoid temptation with his help?"

"That's good," Katherine said, taken aback ever so slightly. "Because temptation is ultimately a selfish act. I'm stealing that one from you."

"Seems like you're the one drawing it out of me. I'll give you full rights and a share of the profits."

"Deal. Now I think it's time we defer to the expert on this next matter.

"Mrs. Violet, what wisdom do you have for Kelli regarding the phrase 'deliver us from evil'?"

"Don't do anything stupid," Mrs. Violet squawked. "If you think you shouldn't be thinking it, don't. If you think you shouldn't be doing it, don't. If you think it's anything but right, it's wrong. And yes, I am the expert. I've seen nine decades of war, disasters, death, and overall debauchery. The world is going to …"

"Accidents, illness, and natural disasters. There you go." Katherine interrupted before Mrs. Violet could make her Hades reference.

"But there's more to it, right?"

"We are all sinners, but you're right. We aren't the root of all evil. What are some other examples?"

"Basically, I'm asking for protection from evil within me and from outside forces. 'Please shield me from worldly ills.'"

"I know you're about to run, but can I tempt you with a cinnamon roll before you head out?"

"Help me to be my best self, Katherine."

"Touché."

Three hours later, Guy strolled through back door.

"Someone got up early this morning," Katherine said sarcastically.

"I just couldn't abandon that bed this morning."

"You missed our surrogate daughter this morning."

"And what did y'all hash out this morning?"

"Let's see if you can pick out exactly which part of the prayer we tackled this morning.

"She is seeking to ask forgiveness in earnest, as in actually improving, altering, and growing. And she's seeking forgiveness as an expression of divine love to help her to be her best self, while asking for protection from evil within her and from outside forces."

"That would be 'forgive us our debts as we forgive our debtors. And lead us not into temptation, but deliver us from evil.' Got it all wrapped up, huh?"

"We both know it's never done, but I'd say she is on the path to clarity."

Kelli's prayer continues ...

Forgive me for the things I think, say, and do that I shouldn't; the things I don't think, say, and do that I should; and the mindsets underneath that prompt these wrong behaviors. I want to repent, reset my thinking, and extend that same spirit to others (Matt. 6:12 NIV).

"Be ye kind to one another, tender-hearted, forgiving one another" (Eph. 4:32 NIV). "Love one another" (John 15:17 MSG). "There abide faith, hope, and charity. The greatest of these is charity" (1Cor. 13:13 KJV)—loving and forgiving, dynamic loving and forgiving, harmonious loving and forgiving.

Lead me to play the next right note—faith notes, home notes, contribution notes to accompany authentic living and divine engagement in my circles of influence (Luke 9:62 MSG). Thank you for my circles—my yet-to-be-found soulmate, my parents, siblings, cousins, and other family circles; my friendship, church, professional, and organizational circles.

Lead us to resist the temptation to focus on ourselves, each other, our challenges; rather, lead us to focus on you and to see our challenges as opportunities to know you more fully, to experience and share you differently (Matt. 6:13 KJV). Lead us to address our challenges with the giants—with the trust of Joseph and Mary (Matt. 1:20 NIV, Luke 1:38 NIV), the clarity of vision of Esther (Est. 4:14–17 NIV), the courage of Joshua (Jos. 1 NIV), the persistence of Jacob (Gen. 29:20–30 NIV), the perseverance of Joseph (Gen. 37–45 NIV). Lead us to build our boats with Noah (Gen. 6:9–22 NIV), climb our mountains with Abraham (Gen. 22:1–8 NIV) in full faith and obedience, experiencing your grace with every step and your strength made perfect in our weakness.

Deliver us from evil, inside and out (Matt. 6:13 NIV). Empower us with the discipline to say no to the obvious wrong choices, the vision and the wisdom to discern between the good and the best, the patience and courage not to settle. Deliver us from accidents, illness, natural disasters, catastrophes, and human harm.

CHAPTER 7

Over the course of the past few weeks, life had interrupted Kelli's weekly visits to Kat's. Amid the sea of out-of-town trips, early morning meetings and workouts, and countless immovable deadlines, Kelli could not find a way back to the cozy coffee cafe.

Essentially, the Kelli version of the Lord's Prayer was in place. Not that it was done. It would never be done. But the structure was there and ready-made for remolding, reshaping, and readjusting with the greatest of ease whenever the need arose.

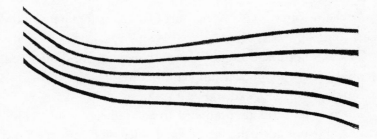

For the most basic of summations for her prayer, she did the following:

- Recognized the vertical relationship with God to start the prayer.
- Sought the vision of heaven and heavenly behavior.
- Held faith that he would provide the necessities.

- Recognized her responsibility to live interdependently with him and share his love.
- Looked for guidance throughout each day.
- Expressed heart-felt thanks for all people in her circles.

Today, her hiatus from Kat's was coming to a close. Having achieved a foundation and methodology through which to pray on a daily basis, Kelli had hit yet another bump in the road.

"Hello there, stranger," Katherine said from her usual table.

Things appeared serene this morning. Pastor John and his youth minister, Debbie, occupied their normal spot by the window, where they were planning out the week's activities. Professor Albert casually perused the latest batch of student essays occupying every inch of a four-seat table, and a couple of earbud-clad collegiate coeds attacked their assignments with a silent ferocity.

"I know, I know," Kelli said. "I've been out of town, working early ... you name it, I've been up to my neck in it."

"I figured the prayer was done and you'd moved on to a chain coffee house."

"A chain coffee house? What sort of soulless ingrate would do such a thing?"

"It was a horrible thing to assume. I apologize and offer you a cup on the house for your triumphant return."

"Apology cup accepted."

The next few minutes produced an amazed Katherine. As Kelli revealed and unfolded the layers she'd integrated into the Lord's Prayer, Katherine became inspired herself.

"You have taken this thing to a level I never expected."

"At this point, it all just kinda makes sense and seems like it was common sense to begin with. I just had to think on it and let the chips fall in line. My latest roadblock hit me this weekend, though. If I know exactly what my day is supposed to look like, then that image is stemming from me and not him."

"How do you make sure it's coming from him?"

Mrs. Violet aloofly burst, as much as the elderly could burst, into the room, pronounced her nourishment request of the moment, and blasted right into the conversation.

"I woke up this morning knowing exactly what was going to happen today."

Kelli, yet again, felt like a player on Katherine's stage of life. As Mrs. Violet rattled on about her typical day, complete with details no one should share, Kelli felt the concept strike her in the head once more.

"And now I'm sitting here waiting an hour for my sandwich."

"Mrs. Violet," Katherine patiently chimed in. "You ordered your sandwich two minutes ago, and Marco already has it toasting."

"Whatever. It wouldn't hurt any one of you to respect your elders a bit more."

With Mrs. Violet's attention turning to Professor Albert, Katherine returned her eyes to Kelli, who was quietly reading through her prayer thoughts with a pleasant smile.

"What just happened?"

"As long as I recognize each day will be different, and I can only respond to the surprises, all I can do is use prayer throughout the day to help guide me through his cues."

"Is that it?"

"He's created each of us to play unique parts in 'his most excellent harmonies.' None of us know which notes to play when, how fast or slow to play them, or how soft or loud. We just have to play them until we get it as close to right as we can in our imperfections."

"And just when I think this couldn't get any better!" Katherine's amazement continued.

"'Thine is the Kingdom, the power, and the glory forever and ever, amen.' Why was it so hard to come to this conclusion? He is the end-all and be-all."

"Mrs. Violet, you are an inspiration," Katherine proclaimed.

"What? I'll tell you what I'm inspired to do. I'm inspired to …"

Marco placed the sandwich neatly in front of her, quelling her desire to berate him any more.

"You were saying?"

"I was saying ..."

Mrs. Violet's attention turned solely to the sandwich as she seemed to forget her surroundings.

"Are you done now?" Katherine asked, knowing the answer.

"In a manner of speaking. The theory and concept are fully in place. All that's left is the execution."

"So, next week? Same bat time, same bat channel?"

"I couldn't imagine anything else!"

Kelli's first version in full:

"Our Father in heaven, hallowed be your name"
*(Matt. 6:9 NIV)—Creator, Eternal Father, God the
Father, God the Son, God the Holy Spirit. What does
that mean? Who am I to honor you? But, then, who
am I not to?*

*You created me. You know me. You love me. You've
accepted me into your eternal family (John 3:16 NIV).
You invite me to join your most excellent harmonies
(Phil. 4:9 MSG). You call me to accompany authentic
living and divine engagement, to be your instrument
playing the parts of soulmate, family member, friend,
advocate, and neighbor.*

*I am your instrument participating in your song,
your symphony, your work.*

*Your kingdom come, your will be done on earth—
through me today—as it is in heaven (Matt.6:10
NIV). What does that mean for me today? Will I be
playing loudly or softly? I don't know what this part
of the song sounds like, and my human eyes can't read
the music. I know who and what are on my agenda,
but I don't know what the people in my life need to
hear from you through me today. That is really fuzzy.
It is such a stretch for me to see myself functioning "as
it is in heaven," where every single thought, word,
and action surely come from love—genuine, selfless,
divine love.*

*So I step into this day the way Peter stepped out
of the boat. With his attentions firmly fixed on you,
Jesus—God the Son, the Living Word, the only life
lived perfectly in love—he walked confidently on
water. His challenge actually became the foundation
for his walk. With my attention on you and alert to*

the passions, intuition, and insights prompted by you, Holy Spirit (John 20:22 NIV), I will walk confidently in my calling today, and my challenging distractions will be mitigated to background music for my parts in your glorious harmonies (Phil. 4:9 MSG).

I want to play my parts today with loving grace and elegance. I look to you to give me all I need to do that, including health, wellness, energy, stamina, ideas, fluency, focus, peace, fun, and an intimate relationship with you (Matt. 6:11 NIV). All that I need to have only those thoughts, conversations, and behaviors that are true, noble, right, pure, lovely, admirable, excellent, and praiseworthy. I want to think on these things and practice these things, and I can with you (Phil. 4:8-9 NIV).

Not as a puppet waiting for you to pull my strings, but with you. You have set me free, giving me freedom of choice (Gal. 5:13-15 MSG). I am free to choose my thoughts, words, and actions, and today I choose to partner with you. I choose to walk with you, work with you, and watch how you do it. I choose to learn from you the unforced rhythms of grace (Matt. 11:28-30 MSG).

I choose to partner with you in exercising vision—anticipating outcomes, results, and consequences of what I think, say, and do, and in forming the next right piece of the picture of my calling (Pro. 29:18 KJV).

I choose to partner with you in focusing and executing my calling today, taking your love in and giving it all away (Matt. 6:30-33 MSG); in loving and forgiving dynamically with a generous spirit (2 Cor. 9:8-11 MSG), knowing you will provide everything I need—all the resources, even time—to play my parts throughout this day with excellence, elegance, and grace (Luke 12:25-32 MSG).

Partnering with you today, I choose to be fully present, listening with genuine consideration and sharing my perceptions with courage—even bold courage—as appropriate (Acts 17:22-31 MSG). I choose to celebrate what's right with people and work with them to share authentic gifts and bents (Rom. 12:4-5 MSG).

And, partnering with you today, I choose to grow—gracefully and continuously—in all facets of my life (Luke 2:52 NIV).

Forgive me for the things I think, say, and do that I shouldn't; the things I don't think, say, and do that I should; and the mindsets underneath that prompt these wrong behaviors. I want to repent, reset my thinking, and extend that same spirit to others (Matt. 6:12 NIV).

"Be ye kind to one another, tender-hearted, forgiving one another" (Eph. 4:32 NIV). "Love one another" (John 15:17 MSG). "There abide faith, hope, and charity. The greatest of these is charity" (1Cor. 13:13 KJV)—loving and forgiving, dynamic loving and forgiving, harmonious loving and forgiving.

Lead me to play the next right note—faith notes, home notes, contribution notes to accompany authentic living and divine engagement in my circles of influence (Luke 9:62 MSG). Thank you for my circles—my yet-to-be-found soulmate, my parents, siblings, cousins, and other family circles; my friendship, church, professional, and organizational circles.

Lead us to resist the temptation to focus on ourselves, each other, our challenges; rather, lead us to focus on you and to see our challenges as opportunities to know you more fully, to experience and share you differently (Matt. 6:13 KJV). Lead us to address our challenges with the giants—with the trust of Joseph and Mary (Matt. 1:20 NIV, Luke 1:38 NIV), the clarity of vision of Esther (Est. 4:14–17 NIV), the courage of Joshua (Jos. 1 NIV), the persistence of Jacob (Gen. 29:20–30 NIV), the perseverance of Joseph (Gen. 37–45 NIV). Lead us to build our boats with Noah (Gen. 6:9–22 NIV), climb our mountains with Abraham (Gen. 22:1–8 NIV) in full faith and obedience, experiencing your grace with every step and your strength made perfect in our weakness.

Deliver us from evil, inside and out (Matt. 6:13 NIV). Empower us with the discipline to say no to the obvious wrong choices, the vision and the wisdom to discern between the good and the best, the patience and courage not to settle. Deliver us from accidents, illness, natural disasters, catastrophes, and human harm.

Lead us to know you created each of us to play unique parts (Romans 12:3–8 KJV) in your most excellent harmonies. I want to participate fully. And because I don't know which note to play when, I will be prayerful throughout this day. In all things with prayer and thanksgiving, I will let my requests be made known to you, and I will accept the peace that comes with knowing you are in charge (Phil. 4:6–7 KJV). You are omnipotent, omniscient, and omnipresent. Thine is the kingdom, the power, and the glory forever (Matt. 6:13 KJV). You always win.

All things do work together for good for those who live in love with you (Rom. 8:28 ASV). Nothing can separate me from your love (Rom. 8:38–39 NIV).

You are the song, the symphony. I am a note, a rest, a key change, a staccato on someone else's note.

As I abide in you and your words abide in me, I can ask whatever I want (John 15:5–8 MSG) and you will answer. Out of your infinite wisdom, love, grace, and mercy, you will answer, and your answer will be perfect.

Amen.

APPENDIX

A Guide for Personalizing the Lord's Prayer

Kelli's challenge was mental paralysis. Sound familiar? Have you ever been stuck like that? Would you like to go forward in the kind of peace that comes from a solid, intimate relationship with our Father?

That the Lord's Prayer could become a personal tool was Kelli's first "aha." She began to use it as her template for daily divine conversations, and as her divine conversations deepened, so did her relationship with her Father. She came to realize the connection between conversation, divine relationship, and inner peace.

The following outline is designed to help you begin your own exploration.

Suggestions:
- Focus on one section for a week or longer.
- Read through all of the questions in that section.
- Pick one or more each day to guide you in finding divine nuggets of truth.
- Write your thoughts in the spaces provided and/or in a notebook or journal.
- Every day, try out your nuggets in a real conversation with God. (He will honor your efforts to deepen your divine relationship.)

To begin, Kelli explores who God is, who she is in him, and how she can honor him authentically.

"Our Father in heaven, hallowed be your name"
(Matt. 6:9 NIV).

Explore who God is to you:
- What's in a name?
- "Our" means you and _____?
- What does the word *father* connote for you?
- Use a Bible app or hard-copy resources to search for names for the Father used in Scripture.
- What do those names suggest about who God is?

```

```

Explore who you are to God:
- What are your names—whole name, name most people use, professional name, nickname, name your mom called you when you were little, etc.?
- What do your names tell you about who you are?
- What is unique about your relationship with God?
- Ask the Father how he views your relationship with him.
- What name for God most represents your current relationship?
- What name represents the relationship you want to have with God?

```

```

Explore whom God is calling you to be:

- How much clarity do you have around your life purpose?
- Search scripture to find how Abraham, David, Isaiah, Mary, Jesus, Paul, and Esther expressed their life purposes or callings.
- Kelli determined her calling as accompanying authentic living and divine engagement. Drawing on a favorite Scripture passage, she identified "musical instrument" as her metaphor. Name a few of your favorite metaphors from Scripture.
- How do you choose to express your calling?
- What would completing the following sentence give you? "God created me to be a _____ (metaphor) and to _____ (two or three verbs ending in *ing*) for _____ (whom)."
- How else might you express your divine calling?
- Kelli identified six roles as current ways to live her calling: his instrument, soulmate, family member, friend, advocate, and neighbor.
- Name five to seven ways you choose to live your calling.
- Investigate the roles lived by three of your biblical heroes over their whole lifetimes.
- How do their examples inform you about your roles?

Personalize this first part of the prayer focusing on who God is, who you are, your relationship to each other, and the calling he has placed on your life.

In this next part, Kelli gains insight into vision and faith. She recognizes herself as part of a much bigger picture that she cannot and will not be able to clearly see.

"Your kingdom come, your will be done on earth—through me today—as it is in heaven" (Matt. 6:10 NIV).

Use these questions to explore the concept of blending your agenda with his:

- What does inserting "through me today" between "earth" and "as" call up for you?
- What would be extraordinary about today if it were as it really is in heaven?
- How would it look, sound, taste, feel, and smell?
- What would you be like?
- What is on your agenda today?
- Consistent with the theme of her purpose statement, Kelli referred to her agenda as a part of his song. How might you choose to express your agenda as a part of his agenda?
- What difference might it make to have a mindset of joining him in his work?
- What would be different about yesterday if it had been as it is in heaven?
- What difference would it make if every word you use today were as it is in heaven?

- What might the people in your life need to hear from God through you today?
- Because it is such a stretch to envision what it is like in heaven, Kelli pictured herself doing what Peter did when he got out of the boat—focusing on Jesus and on the promptings of the Holy Spirit. What happened when Peter did that?
- Read that story from Matthew 14:28–30 (MSG). What happened when Peter lost his focus?
- What story from Scripture inspires you to visualize your life purpose?
- What is it about that story that speaks to you?
- Picture yourself in that story. How might it help you create and sustain a vision of you living today as if you were in heaven?

Personalize this part of your prayer, focusing on vision and on the faith required to step into the picture of what it will be like to live your calling today.

Embracing uncertainties and lack of complete clarity, Kelli recognizes she must ask for what she needs to live her calling and be dependent on the Trinity to provide her daily needs.

"I look to you to give me all I need to do that, including: health, wellness, energy, stamina, ideas, fluency, focus, peace, fun, and an intimate relationship with you" (Matt. 6:11 NIV).

Explore ways to express your daily needs:
- What do you need to live your calling today?
- Read 2 Corinthians 9:8-11 (MSG). What does it tell you?
- Brainstorm a long, comprehensive list of your daily needs.
- Bundle similar needs together.
- Prioritize the bundles.
- Name the bundles.
- Read Philippians 4:8–9 (NIV).

Personalize this part of the prayer, focusing on asking for what you need, knowing he will provide what you need to live your calling today.

Having recognized her dependence on him for her needs, Kelli's next "aha" is that she has responsibility in using what he provides, that she is not a puppet but has freedom of choice. Furthermore, she can partner with him, using what he provides, to live her calling each day. Kelli begins this section by owning her choices and then proceeds to clarify choices for the purpose of aligning her living with her deepest values.

"I am free to choose my thoughts, words, and actions, and today I choose to partner with you" (Matt. 11:28-30 MSG).

Explore what it means to have freedom of choice:

- Do a Scripture search on your Bible app or a hard-copy source for *responsibility.*
- What does that give you?
- How do you choose to express the way you will put his provisions into practice?
- Read Matthew 11:28–30 (MSG). What does it say to you about interdependence?
- Name twenty-five values. Eliminate about half. Eliminate about half again. Prioritize what's left.
- What Scripture helps to clarify each of your values?
- Kelli used "I choose" statements and referenced Scripture to clarify her values. For example, she identified authenticity to be one of her core values and chose to express it as "I choose to celebrate what's right with people and work with them to share authentic gifts and bents" (Romans 12:4-5 MSG).
- Complete this or a similar statement for each of your values. "I choose to be interdependent with you in _____."

Personalize this part of the prayer with a focus on partnering with Jesus to lead yourself.

It is here that Kelli puts words around her limited capacity and her responsibility to reach out to others in love. In doing so, she gains deeper understanding about what love actually means.

Kelli chooses language to represent both present and future in asking forgiveness.

> "Forgive me for the things I think, say, and do that I shouldn't; the things I don't think, say, and do that I should; and the mindsets underneath that prompt these wrong behaviors" (Matt. 6:12 NIV).
> - How do you choose to ask him to forgive you?
> - What Scripture do you want to use to ground your request for forgiveness?

```


```

Draft this part of your prayer, your divine conversation personal.

```


```

Next, Kelli's focus lands on *love* as a choice, a verb.

> "Be ye kind to one another, tender-hearted, forgiving one another" (Eph. 4:32 NIV).

Express your thoughts around love.

```


```

Explore forgiveness:
- How are forgiveness and love related?
- Regarding the act or process of forgiveness, what Scripture holds insight and inspiration for you?
- How will you express your commitment to extend forgiveness to others?

Continuing to think of love as a choice, Kelli turns her thoughts to serving those in her circles—her yet-to-be-found soulmate, family, friends, church, professional, and organizational circles—through her life calling.

"Lead me to play the next right note" (Luke 9:62 MSG).

Explore connections between your life calling and your life circles:
- What is your calling?
- Use a phrase or a sentence that best calls it to mind for you.
- Connect your calling to the people you feel led to impact.
- Express thanks to him for your calling and those people and organizations you influence.

Recognizing that temptation challenges her circles, Kelli includes them in asking for strength to resist. She adds meaning by referencing specific strengths involved in resisting temptation as well as biblical heroes who modeled these strengths for us.

"Lead us to resist the temptation to …" (Matt. 6:13 KJV).

Explore temptation:
- What are some ways you are currently experiencing temptation?
- How might you look at them in a positive way?
- What would that give you?

```
┌─────────────────────────────────────────┐
│                                         │
│                                         │
│                                         │
│                                         │
└─────────────────────────────────────────┘
```

Drawing from your thoughts and ideas about temptation, draft this part of your divine conversation.

```
┌─────────────────────────────────────────┐
│                                         │
│                                         │
│                                         │
└─────────────────────────────────────────┘
```

Kelli gives evil two designations—within us and outside of us. She chooses to ask for deliverance from both kinds.

"Deliver us from evil, inside and out" (Matt. 6:13 NIV).

Explore the ways that evil impacts your life and those in your circles:
- What does inside evil bring up for you?
- What does outside evil bring up for you?

- What do you choose to ask him to give you to combat inside evil?
- What do you choose to ask him to give you to combat outside evil?

[blank box]

Experiencing a rich, comprehensive conversation with God up to this point, Kelli chooses to commit to living her authentic calling today.

"Lead us to know you created each of us to ..."
(Romans 12:3-8 KJV).

Explore commitment options for today:
- You are the only you there has ever been or ever will be. God created you to _____ unique _____.
- What will you commit to do today so you won't miss your supply of joy?

[blank box]

Draft this part of your divine conversation.

[blank box]

Kelli goes full circle as she comes back to recognizing who God is and who she is in him.

"Thine is the kingdom, the power, and the glory forever" (Matt. 6:13 KJV).

"All things do work together for good" (Rom. 8:28 ASV).

Reflect on your learning:
- What are you aware of now that you weren't prior to personalizing the Lord's Prayer?
- What do you still need to learn?

Though the template stays the same, Kelli's prayer is different every day. Some parts, like her purpose statement and her roles, are stable, though she absolutely remains open to changing them as she feels divinely led to do so. Some parts, like envisioning what her agenda might look like in heaven, change daily. Some days, she goes through the whole conversation early in the morning. Some days, she only does one part by noon because of a time crunch or because she is letting herself process an idea or question.

Create next steps:
- As you ponder what you are going to do with this prayer, consider these suggestions:
  - Commit to spending one twenty-minute block of time each week to search Scripture, reflect on sermons, listen to divine guidance, and draft a few words or lines of your personal Lord's Prayer conversation.

- In what part of the day will you most often focus on your divine conversation?
- Use what you draft as soon as you draft it and let it grow from there.

Through personalizing the Lord's Prayer, Kelli shook loose from her mental paralysis and found a sense of peace beyond any she had known before. Perhaps more significant is that she developed a habit of initiating powerful personal conversations with her Heavenly Father every day. Though her prayers are never the same from one day to the next, her basic structure stays consistent and serves to deepen her divine relationship and provide ongoing peace about who she is and how she is living her life.

Printed in the United States
By Bookmasters